feel

PAGE PUBLISHING, INC.
New York, NY

First originally published by Page Publishing, Inc. 2018

ISBN 978-1-64138-724-8 (Hardcover)
ISBN 978-1-64138-723-1 (Digital)

Printed in the United States of America

feel

To: MORENA,
FEEL AND SHARE OFTEN !

Cris

Cristi DeFino
author • artist

To Marni and Ryan,
My heroes and my inspiration.

You are strong
and beautiful and loving
and kind.

And your hearts feel.

No wind or storm or cloud
is more powerful than that.

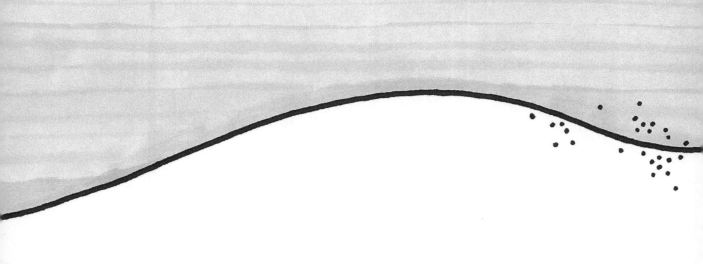

And to my mom,
who first taught my heart to feel.
Thank you.

One day, Myrin asked Windy, "Do you think I'm good enough?
My heart feels big, but when you're around, I feel small."
Windy said, "You ARE small and weak.
Look at how I can blow you over."

Myrin walked away.

A few years later, Myrin met Sunny, who lived in a big sand box. Sunny called it "the garden."

Myrin asked Sunny, "How does the garden get so big?"
Sunny said, "Windy helps out.
But mostly the garden grows when my heart feels."

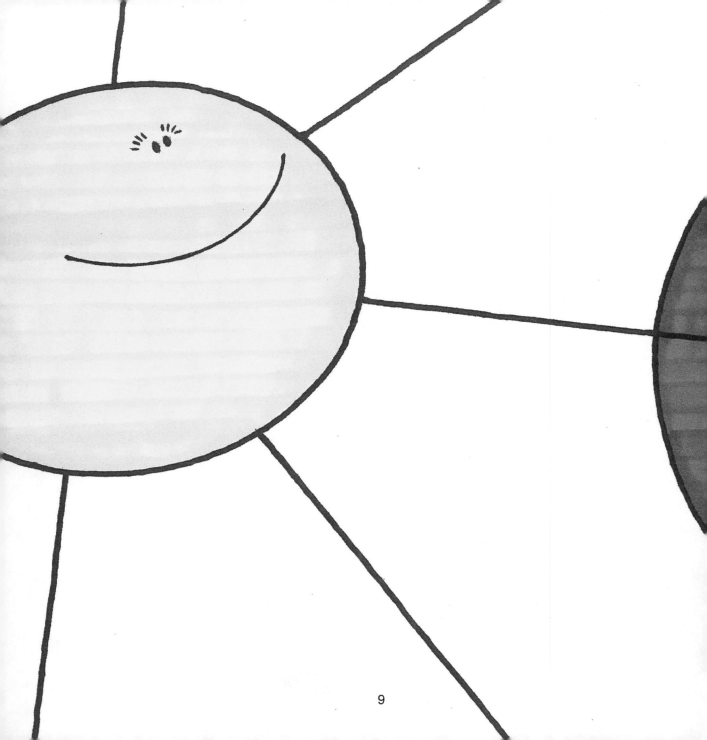

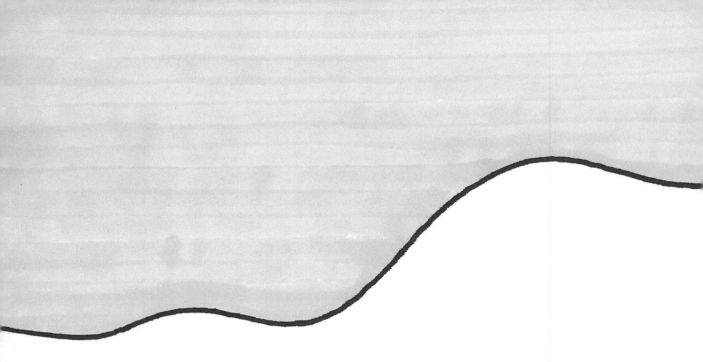

The three became friends.
They did fun things together and played and made
everyone laugh.
They hugged a lot.
They waved at big people and smiled at small people.
They built castles together and invited
everyone into their
sand garden.

When they felt sad or angry or scared or lonely, they sat
together in their big garden and let their hearts feel.
They shared their feelings and talked through things with
each other.
Sometimes, they played ping pong.

And the garden grew.

And Myrin no longer felt small around Windy.

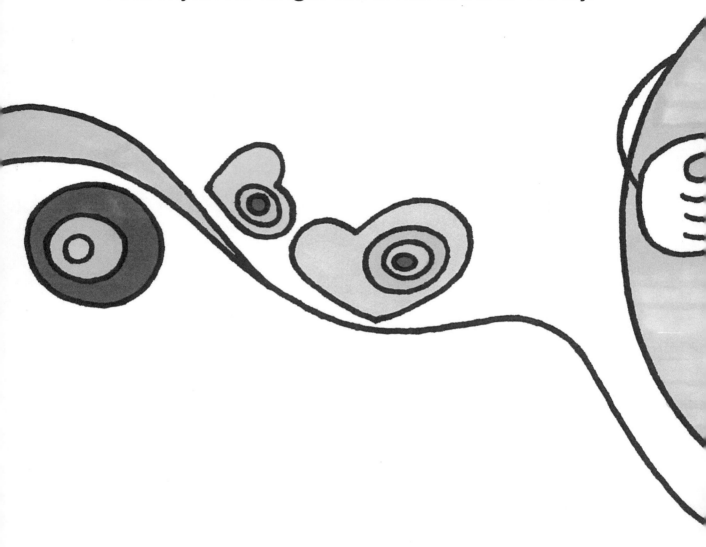

One day, Myrin asked Sunny,
"Do you think I'm good enoug
My heart feels big,
but when you're not around
I feel small."

19